Swooshing bodies start to bang,
Slamming sneakers start to skid—
The ball starts and never stops,
Moving smooth and sweet
From man to man to . . . Mike!

Philomel Books · New York

Jump!

from the life of
Michael Jordan

FLOYD COOPER

For "Coach" Lenwood Edwards,
Greensboro, North Carolina.

Special thanks:
To Maria Lewis, media specialist at
Edge Elementary School in Niceville, Florida.
Your assistance with biographical materials was timely.
And to Christopher Christian, a cool friend
and perfect model. Thanks for being "like Mike."

LETTER TO THE READER

Michael Jordan's life will be, for a long time to come, one that exemplifies winning. Reaching the highest levels of endeavor, Michael "Air" Jordan's life story is the life story of a champion.

However, the lessons for the young are in Air Jordan's formative years, the early years. Away from the blinding glare of stardom, one can better see how the seeds of determination and "hating to lose" became the backbone of his persistence and his meeting the challenges to "step up"! This is not to dissect and examine how to be great, but simply to suggest that with perseverance and determination, a greatness may be within reach of us all.

—Floyd Cooper

His name was Michael, and from the time he was a little boy, he always seemed to be in and out of mischief. His parents did their best to keep all of the Jordan kids busy at their home in Wallace, North Carolina. James Ronald and Deloris, Larry and Roslyn—those kids couldn't have been happier playing sports and games. But Michael? He just had a different kind of energy, and curiosity, too.

Like the time his daddy told him, "Don't touch the ax," and Michael heard him say, plain as day, "Don't touch the ax!" But he took the ax anyway, and behind the house he began to chop. Chop! Chop! Chop! It wasn't long before that ax came down on his five-year-old toe.

The Jordans kept on trying. Five kids aren't easy! Along with sports, they gave all the children rules and chores to keep them plenty busy. But there just weren't enough rules or chores to match the boundless bustle of those Jordan kids. They bounced off the walls of their bungalow home. And young Michael was the bounciest.

Maybe, the Jordans figured, if they moved to another house, with more room and space.

And that's what they did. When Michael was seven years old, the Jordans moved to suburban Wilmington, North Carolina. Michael's mom and dad even let the kids help build the house so they could learn how working together as a team was the way to get things done—and so they could get rid of some of that energy.

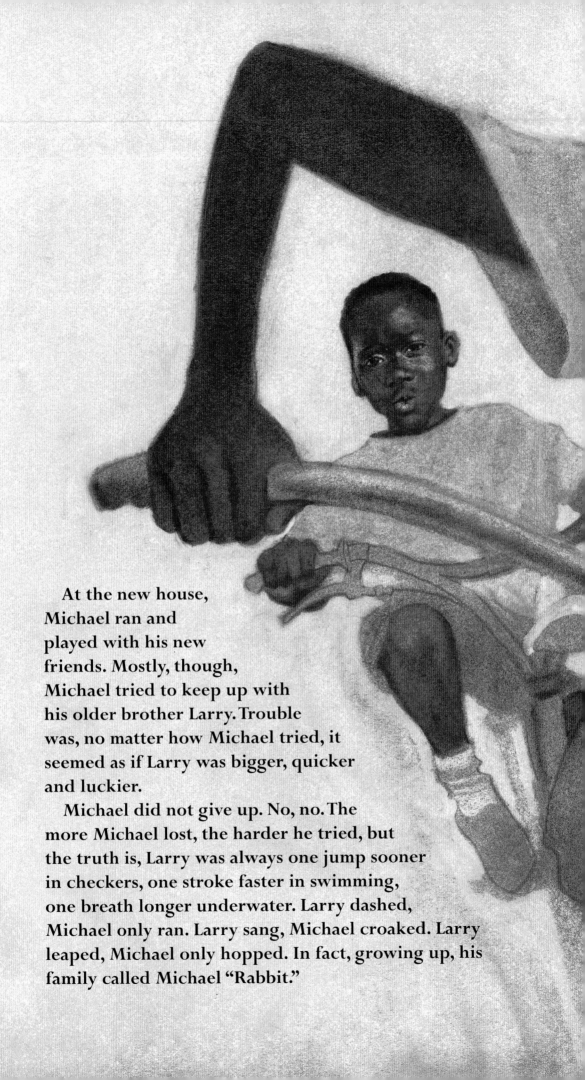

At the new house,
Michael ran and
played with his new
friends. Mostly, though,
Michael tried to keep up with
his older brother Larry. Trouble
was, no matter how Michael tried, it
seemed as if Larry was bigger, quicker
and luckier.

Michael did not give up. No, no. The
more Michael lost, the harder he tried, but
the truth is, Larry was always one jump sooner
in checkers, one stroke faster in swimming,
one breath longer underwater. Larry dashed,
Michael only ran. Larry sang, Michael croaked. Larry
leaped, Michael only hopped. In fact, growing up, his
family called Michael "Rabbit."

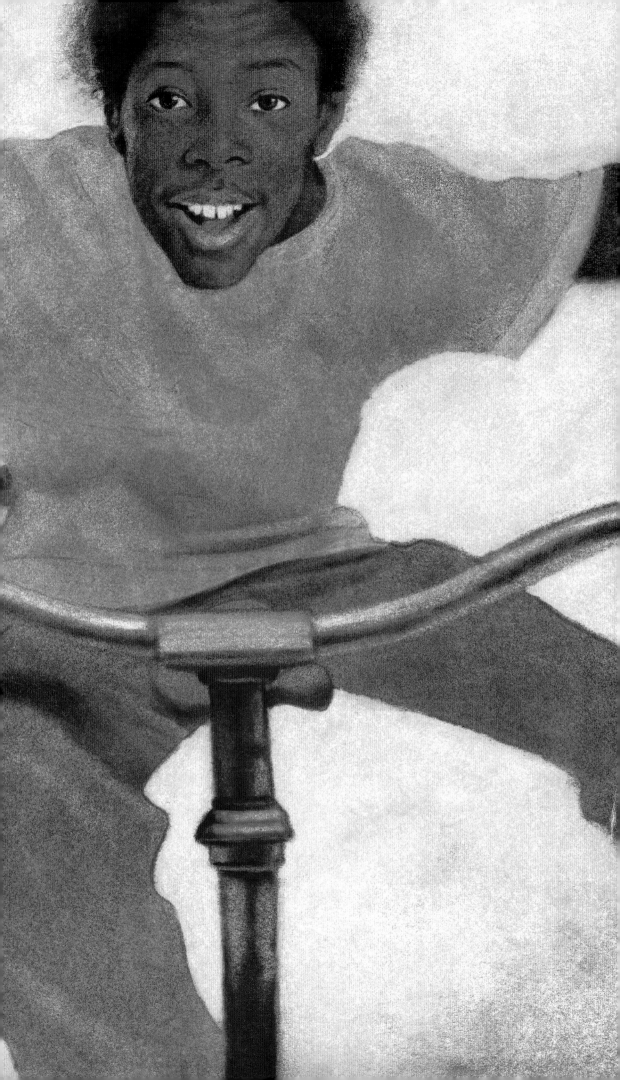

One of the first things that Michael's father had done at the new house was to put up a basketball hoop right in the backyard. Kids from all over would play on that hoop. But more and more—after the other kids had gone—the games ended up being a contest between Larry and Michael. They would play one-on-one so much that the grass underneath the hoop refused to grow from the pounding.

Michael wasn't growing much, either! So he started hanging by his arms from a swing set for hours each day, hoping to stretch himself taller. But it was no use. For all too many years, Michael was still only "Rabbit."

Now, Michael knew there was only one way for him to play basketball better than Larry, and that was to play more. He looked to pick up games on the blacktop at school or in the park. Or after he'd lose to Larry, he'd play alone, pounding and sweating and working that poor little backyard court like his sharecropper grandpa worked the soil—from daybreak to day's end.

And he wouldn't stop until he heard the screen door spring and his father's voice saying, "Come in now, son, time for bed."

Just when he discovered the game at Laney High School is hard to say. But the sun seemed hotter there, the moves seemed quicker on the full blacktop court there, the hoops seemed higher—and the game seemed better to eleven-year-old Michael. The raw power of the springy older players as they shot the ball and talked trash in the hot, salty breeze, now that was something to see and hear. What did he want? Why, he wanted to be asked to play.

But for what seemed like a long time, he did little more than wish.

Time helps. And it helped Michael. By the time he was in junior high, he was turning out to be a fair baseball player. In fact, when he was twelve, he led his baseball team to the state championship!

Grew smarter, too, persuading his friends to do some of his dreaded chores, like mowing the lawn, and leaving him to do only the ones he enjoyed, like ironing his own shirts. And he began to grow taller, taller than anyone in his family.

Hanging on the swing set must have helped.

One thing Michael always had time for was friends, and he had friends of many different backgrounds and cultures. His best friend was a white boy named David, and he hadn't given much thought to color until one day when he and David went to a swimming pool party and were surprised when Michael turned out to be the only black kid there.

Michael was even more surprised when he jumped into the pool and all the white kids got out. He decided he didn't want to be where he wasn't welcome, and left the party. Michael knew he had a true friend when David left with him.

Despite all the baseball that was going down, by the time he was in high school, Michael started to live and breathe basketball. He loved everything about it—the smell of the ball, the swoosh of the net. Soon it was all he wanted to play. He even gave up baseball. He saw less and less of Larry these days because Larry was becoming a true sports star—he was too busy to play with his little brother. More and more Michael hung out at the blacktop by the high school.

One day, the blacktop kids asked him to play. There was a crowd gathered by the fence, boys and girls, but this was Michael's chance!

Suddenly Michael had the ball. He dribbled it down the court, taking that ball hard to the hole, and just as he reached the rim—bam! A huge body slammed into Michael. From the hot tack tar, he looked up at the ball as it bounced off the rim. Michael had blown the layup.

From the side a voice broke the slo-mo silence in a teasing, mocking whine. "Hey, Ears, open your eyes." Michael gritted himself back into the game, but the taunts began to spread from the onlookers.

With each dribble, he was scoffed at for his "little boy" haircut and the way his ears stuck out. With every layup he was jeered about the way his tongue hung out of his mouth when he shot the ball. And right in front of the girls!

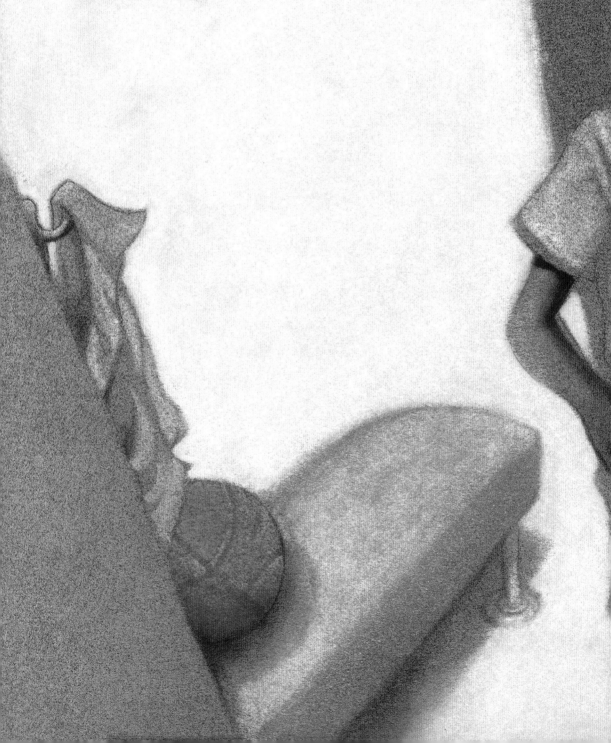

None of it stopped Michael. He came back and played the next day, and the next. And the next. And the truth is, he got better and better. Finally one day, he and his buddy Leroy decided to try out for the Laney High School varsity basketball team. Surely he would make it—Larry had.

But at the end of the week, when the list of players was put up, there was no "Michael Jordan" on it. Even Leroy had made the team.

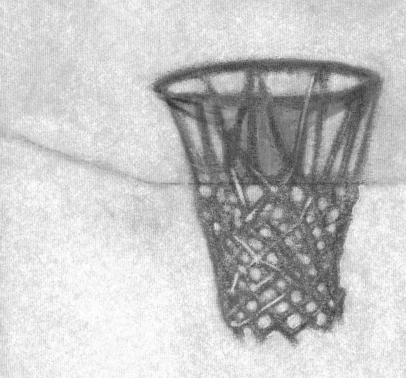

But Coach Herring had seen something he liked in the plucky kid. He put him on the junior varsity team and offered to coach Michael one-to-one if Michael would meet him before school every morning at 6:00 A.M. Michael not only came, he worked hard, dribbling, passing, shooting. Dribbling, passing, shooting. Shooting, shooting. And Michael began to get not just okay, but good.

He got so good, in fact, that the varsity players started coming to all the junior varsity games to watch Michael play.

We don't know exactly when Michael
turned the tables on Larry for the first
time, but it may very well have happened
the summer that Michael shot up four
inches and went to basketball camp. One
afternoon, the two started going at
it again on the backyard hoop.

At first, it seemed just like old times. Family and friends gathered around the hot, sticky court to watch the two brothers. But something was different. When Larry dashed across the court—Michael was there. Larry leaped for the hoop—Michael was there, too.

Soon the brothers were in the thick of the game, a tangle of arms and legs flashing around the orange ball. Could Michael actually win? Larry wasn't worried; he was ahead of Michael by one point. Larry grinned. It was the usual end to the usual game.

Then Michael had the ball. They both knew what usual meant: Michael would leap to dunk and Larry would jump higher, grab it and dunk it for the win. Well, Michael leaped, just like always. And Larry leaped, just like always. But Michael kept going and going, past the wide span of Larry's hands!

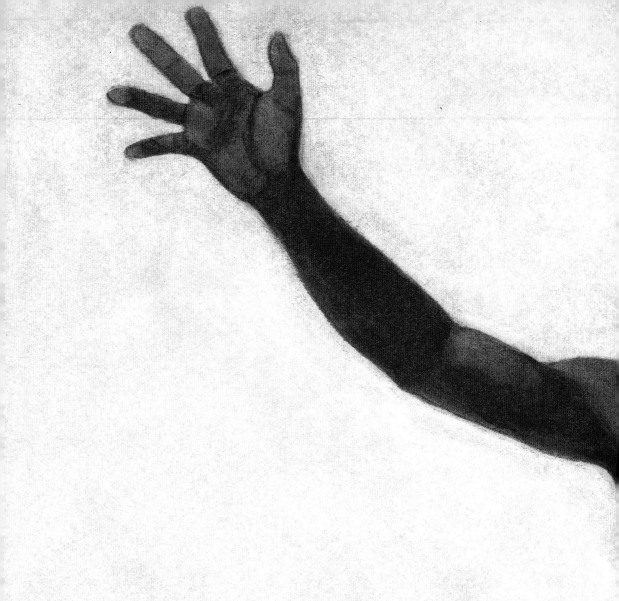

It seemed as if Michael just hung there
for a moment. As if waiting. Was it possible
he had outjumped the master?

He had, and he dunked the ball in the hoop for the win. Michael smiled. He had beaten his brother, the best, at his own game.

The laughing and hand-slapping that followed that magical game followed Michael Jordan—Rabbit—through his entire career. From basketball camps to college teams, and finally into the professional world of basketball, the NBA.

And Larry was there, too, always an athlete in his own right, but rooting for his best competitor. Brothers, friends: whatever Michael Jordan became had started at their backyard hoop, with Larry, with games that went on past dark, that pushed Michael Jordan to become more than he was. And more than any basketball player has ever been in all time.

BIOGRAPHICAL NOTE

Michael Jeffrey Jordan was born on February 17, 1963, in Brooklyn, New York, where his family was staying while his dad completed a training school for General Electric. As a testament to how close-knit they were, the whole family was there: his father, James; his mother, Deloris; his brothers, James Ronald and Larry; and his sister, Deloris. Shortly after Michael was born, the family moved back home to Wallace, North Carolina, where little sister Roslyn was born.

Michael started his remarkable journey to stardom by failing! He failed to make the varsity basketball team at Laney High School. But he didn't quit. He worked hard on the junior varsity team, eventually got a chance to play for the varsity team and led them to the championship. He went on to attend the University of North Carolina, where he led that team to three Atlantic Coast Conference championships and a National Collegiate Athletic Association championship.

Michael's fame continued to bloom as he thrilled old fans and made new fans for basketball with each game he played. When he was invited to try out for the 1984 U.S. Olympic team, the whole world would get the chance to witness Michael's remarkable talents as he helped win the gold medal for the USA. But first, Michael made the decision to leave college and join the National Basketball Association.

The Chicago Bulls were elated when it was their turn to select in the NBA draft and Michael Jordan was still available. Choosing third, they signed Michael to a seven-year contract. Michael had begun his professional career. Watching Michael play was quickly becoming a favorite pastime for more and more sports fans. Nearly every game he would perform some amazing move on the court, whether it was a twisting slash to the hoop to score or an incredible takeoff from the free-throw line to slam down a tomahawk dunk! The Chicago Bulls improved each year, as did Michael's personal trophy case. From rookie-year honors to scoring titles and All-Star teams, to Slam Dunk champion and Most Valuable Player awards, Michael proved his worthiness as a champion.

But with all of these accomplishments, the Bulls and Michael still had not won an NBA championship. That all changed in the 1990–91 basketball season, when the Bulls, led by Michael, became NBA champions! Michael would go on in his stellar career acquiring more honors, including another Olympic gold medal and five more NBA championships.

Michael retired from the game and came back twice in the 1990s. First, in 1994, he took some time off from basketball due to a family tragedy. (He spent that season playing minor-league baseball for the Birmingham Barons, an affiliate of the Chicago White Sox.) Then, after the 1997–98 basketball season, Michael retired from the game a second time. He passed his time in the front office of the Washington Wizards before finally joining the team as a player in 2001. Michael Jordan was back again! He played for two years, retiring for good in 2003. He left the game with many records intact, including career achievements of six NBA championships, five MVP awards, thirteen All-Star games, and scoring 32,292 points!

Even if Michael Jordan never plays in the NBA again, his presence on the court will live on in the spirit and eyes of the players that follow. Mike's presence will be there inside all of those little "like Mikes" who grow up to become stars. Yes, there will be basketball players greater than Michael Jordan, but they will owe that greatness to Michael Jordan and the impact he had on their development. Just as Michael owes those who came before him, like his brother Larry.

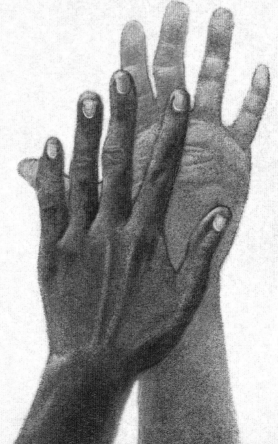

BIBLIOGRAPHY

Christopher, Matt. *On the Court with . . . Michael Jordan*. Boston: Little, Brown and Company, 1996.

Kempf, Don, and James D. Stern, directors. *Michael Jordan to the Max*. VHS. Twentieth Century Fox Corporation, 2000.

Naughton, Jim. *Taking to the Air: The Rise of Michael Jordan*. New York: Warner Books, 1993.

Patricia Lee Gauch, editor

Copyright © 2004 by Floyd Cooper
All rights reserved. This book, or parts thereof, may not be reproduced in any form without permission in writing from the publisher,
PHILOMEL BOOKS
a division of Penguin Young Readers Group,
345 Hudson Street, New York, NY 10014.
Philomel Books, Reg. U.S. Pat. & Tm. Off. The scanning, uploading and distribution of this book via the Internet or via any other means without the permission of the publisher is illegal and punishable by law. Please purchase only authorized electronic editions, and do not participate in or encourage electronic piracy of copyrighted materials.
Your support of the author's rights is appreciated.
Published simultaneously in Canada.   Manufactured in China by South China Printing Co. Ltd.

Designed by Semadar Megged.   Text set in 15-point Perpetua Bold.   The art was done in umber washes of oil, subtracted with an eraser and tinted with mild glazes of mixed media.

Library of Congress Cataloging-in-Publication Data
Cooper, Floyd.   Jump! : from the life of Michael Jordan / Floyd Cooper.   p. cm.   1. Jordan, Michael, 1963– —Juvenile literature. 2. Basketball players—United States—Biography—Juvenile literature. [1. Jordan, Michael, 1963– —Childhood and youth. 2. Basketball players. 3. African Americans—Biography.] I. Title.   GV884.J67C66 2004   796.323'092—dc22   2003025071

ISBN 0-399-24230-9
1 3 5 7 9 10 8 6 4 2
First Impression